LOOK AND FIND®

Disney's
TREASURE PLANET

Illustrated by Art Mawhinney

Cover illustration by
the Disney Storybook Artists

© 2002 Disney Enterprises, Inc.

Visit our Web site at
www.disneybooks.com

Published by
Louis Weber, C.E.O.
Publications International, Ltd.
7373 North Cicero Avenue
Lincolnwood, Illinois 60712

www.pubint.com

Manufactured in China.

8 7 6 5 4 3 2 1

ISBN 0-7853-6997-X

Look and Find is a registered trademark
of Publications International, Ltd.

 publications international, ltd.

This is one day that Jim would rather be building a solar surfer than helping his mother run the Benbow Inn. Can you find Jim? Look for his solar tools, too, because he's going to need them as soon as this rush is over.

Jim

quasar conductor

blade bender

torque adjuster

winch driver

mach override tester

bit pierce

bone weights

crease welder

Jim has managed to unlock the mysterious sphere given to him by Billy Bones. It's a holographic map of the etherium! Use the map to find the way to Treasure Planet and these other intergalactic landmarks.

Coral Galaxy

The Planet Pelsinore

Calyan Abyss

Cygnus Cross

Proteus One

Montressor

Zandaria

Treasure Planet

Magellanic Cloud

Welcome to the spaceport! Jim and Dr. Doppler are ready to embark on the expedition to find Treasure Planet. Look around to find them, as well as these other members of the *Legacy* crew, as they prepare to board the ship.

Silver and Morph

Aquanoggin

Turnbuckle

Meltdown

Scroop

Onus

Birdbrain Mary

Oxy and Moron

Mr. Arrow

Neither Silver nor Jim expected to find these ingredients tucked away in the galley hold of the RLS *Legacy*. Can you find the stuff of which their new friendship is made?

recipe for friendship

a dash of humor

a pound of patience

an opportunity

a cup of kindness

an ounce of respect

honesty

Thanks to Silver, it seems Jim is going to make a fine spacer after all. If this really is the life for him, Jim will be needing a few things. Can you find these spacer things aboard the RLS *Legacy*?

semaphore flag

hornpipe

concertina

sextant

bos'n's whistle

telescope

compass

ship's log

mop and bucket

Mutiny on the *Legacy*! Jim, Dr. Doppler, and Captain Amelia depart in such a hurry that they leave some things behind.

a picture of Jim's mother

Dr. Doppler's expedition suit

Jim's extra socks

Captain Amelia's keys to the brig

Captain Amelia's quill and inkwell

Captain Amelia's chart chest

Dr. Doppler's toothbrush

Dr. Doppler's telescope

Jim's practice knot

Jim, Dr. Doppler, and Captain Amelia are happy to find a hiding place in the tower that B.E.N. calls home. But it's a bit messy. Look around and find these souvenirs B.E.N. collected on his travels with Captain Flint.

Capital of Zandaria commemorative spoon

Coral Galaxy pennant

First Governor of Pelsinore

t-shirt from Montressor

Magellanic Cloud dome

kahfay cup from the Calyan Abyss

Cygnus Cross pencil sharpener

Proteus One foam finger

golden leaf from Treasure Planet

The loot of a thousand worlds! Jim, Silver, and the others have finally made their way to the center of Treasure Planet. Search through the glittering mountains of riches to find these famous plundered treasures.

Flaxxan urn

red diamond of No

blue Priian pearls

Orb of Gentu

sword of Jack Cavanaugh

Ankh of Tarr

figurehead from the *Eleanor Soo*

portrait of Princess Kayla

Go back to the Benbow Inn to find these loyal customers:

- ❏ Mrs. Greene
- ❏ Bubbles Gumm
- ❏ Scot N. Skurt
- ❏ Dr. Beakbill
- ❏ I. M. Flatt
- ❏ I. M. Flatt, Jr. (Little Matt, to his friends)
- ❏ Rose Abovital

Go back to Dr. Doppler's observatory to look for these crazy cosmic things:

- ❏ a movie star
- ❏ a moon pie
- ❏ a sunflower
- ❏ a starfish
- ❏ a falling star
- ❏ a black hole
- ❏ a big dipper

Go back to the spaceport to look for crew members on their way to other ships:

- ❏ Finnbar McPhish
- ❏ Cogg
- ❏ Bluebeard
- ❏ Slugg
- ❏ Two-Ton Tess
- ❏ Dino
- ❏ Snakeyes
- ❏ Queenie B.

Go back to the galley to find these strange foods that Jim has never seen or tasted:

- ❏ bonzaburger
- ❏ purp cream cone
- ❏ hatching-day cake
- ❏ Zirellian jellyworm pizza
- ❏ rootabeer float
- ❏ flame dog
- ❏ korb on the cob

Go back to the RLS *Legacy* under full sail to look for these knots tied by Jim:

❑ clover knot
❑ love me knot
❑ spaghetti knot
❑ lasso knot
❑ square knot
❑ shoelace knot
❑ figure-eight knot

Return to the scene of the mutiny. Can you find 9 skulls and crossbones, left as clues to the pirates' plans?

Go back to the center of Treasure Planet to look for these golden things:

❑ golden goose
❑ golden eagle
❑ goldy-locks
❑ golden fleece
❑ golden egg
❑ golden retriever
❑ golden rule

B.E.N. may be missing his memory chip, but he has just about everything else. Go back to B.E.N.'s place to find these everyday items:

❑ toilet plunger
❑ dustpan
❑ kitchen sink
❑ egg
❑ ball of yarn